ROB CHILDS

THE BIG FREEZE

Illustrated by Aidan Potts

YOUNG CORGI BOOKS

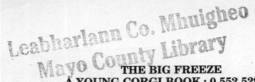

THE BIG FREEZE
A YOUNG CORGI BOOK : 0 552 529672

First published in Great Britain

PRINTING HISTORY
Young Corgi edition published 1997

5 7 9 10 8 6 4

Copyright © Rob Childs, 1997
Illustrations copyright © Aidan Potts, 1997
Cover illustration by Steve Noon

The right of Rob Childs to be identified as the author of
this work has been asserted in accordance with the
Copyright, Designs and Patents Act 1988

Set in 14/18pt Linotype New Century Schoolbook by
Phoenix Typesetting, Ilkley, West Yorkshire.

Young Corgi Books are published by Transworld Publishers Ltd,
61–63 Uxbridge Road, Ealing, London W5 5SA,
in Australia by Transworld Publishers,
c/o Random House Australia Pty Ltd,
20 Alfred Street, Milsons Point, NSW 2061,
in New Zealand by Transworld Publishers,
c/o Random House New Zealand,
18 Poland Road, Glenfield, Auckland,
and in South Avrica by Transworld Publishers,
c/o Random House (Pty) Ltd,
Endulini, 5a Jubilee Road, Parktown 2193

Made and printed in Great Britain by
Mackays of Chatham plc, Chatham, Kent

*Especially for Dad —
simply the best!*

1 Frozen Up

'Have a crack! Hit it!'

Pud didn't really need any such encouragement – least of all from the goalkeeper in his direct line of fire. If there was one thing Pud was good at, it was hitting a football.

So he hit it – hard. Not quite one of his megapower master-blasters, as teammates at Danebridge Primary School called them, but still fierce enough to send defenders diving for cover.

Chris Weston, team captain and goalie, might have told Pud to shoot, but he wasn't *that* stupid. He made no attempt to block it either. He didn't want to risk injury in a knockabout game in the village hall.

Chris let the ball whistle past him and watched it fly wide of the cone too. 'Close! Bad luck, Pud,' he cried out.

'Good shot, David,' praised Mr Jones, resisting the temptation to use the boy's nickname. 'Always worth a pop at goal from there.'

'I'll have a pop from anywhere,' Pud muttered under his breath, cross that he hadn't scored.

'Take a break now, boys,' the headmaster told them.

Most of the players trooped off for a drink of water, but David Bakewell waddled over to a long wooden bench and slumped against the wall. He was joined by his captain.

'Budge up a bit, Pud.'

'What do you mean by that?' he scowled. 'There's plenty of room, I'm not that fat.'

'I never said you were,' Chris defended himself. 'I just want to get to my bag under the bench.'

Like everyone else, Chris had to be a

little wary of Pud's fiery temper. Nothing lit the striker's short fuse quicker than a remark about his size, intentional or otherwise.

'Want a crisp?' Chris asked as he took a packet out of his sports bag.

'What flavour?'

'Smoky bacon.'

'Right, yeah, thanks,' Pud mumbled, pulling out a podgy handful and stuffing them all into his mouth at the same time.

'Would it have mattered what flavour they were?'

'Not really,' Pud spluttered and then grinned. 'I like 'em all.'

'So I've noticed,' Chris sighed, tucking in himself before Pud fancied any second helpings.

'Just look at Carrot-Top!' snorted

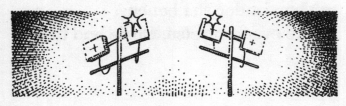

Pud. 'Still dribbling himself daft round all them cones over there.'

They watched little Jamie Robertson waltzing through a line of cones, the ball almost glued to his feet. It wasn't only his red hair that caught the eye. It was his dazzling, twinkle-toed footwork. Despite being two years younger than most of the team, Jamie's speed and tricky ball skills down the wing had produced many of Danebridge's goals so far that season.

The crackly sound of a transistor radio distracted them. 'Huh!' Pud grunted. 'Jonesy stopped the game just to hear the weather forecast!'

'Shut up and listen,' said Chris, hoping for a let-up in the worst winter weather that even his watching grandad could remember.

'The big freeze continues . . .' began

the lady's voice and Chris groaned. It had been the same message for weeks. The deep snow had been fun in the Christmas holidays, but now everywhere was covered with hard-packed ice and he was fed up with all the short, dark, bitterly cold days.

Even worse was the fact that the freezing weather was wrecking their soccer season. It was nearly the end of January and they hadn't played a proper match for two months.

'We're going to have a massive fixture pile-up at this rate.'

'Yeah,' Pud agreed, 'and that won't do our chances of winning the league any good, will it?'

Chris shivered. 'Brrr! It's cold in here tonight too. We should have kept on the move like Jamie.'

'Skinny kids daren't stop or they turn to icicles,' Pud laughed.

Chris went to speak to Grandad. 'No sign of a thaw yet, I gather. By the time we see any grass again, it'll be the cricket season.'

Grandad chuckled. 'Aye, and then it'll probably rain every day!'

When the headmaster restarted the game, Jamie wasted no time in testing out Chris's reflexes. His low, skidding shot took a slight deflection, but the keeper threw himself across the mat to turn the ball away.

'Thought I'd beat you there,' smiled Jamie.

'He wouldn't have smelt it, if I'd whacked it,' Pud boasted. 'Your shots are too weedy.'

Jamie shrugged. 'At least mine are on target!'

The practice continued at half-pace, the novelty of playing indoors having long worn off. The dimly lit, draughty room was far from ideal, but it was the only place they had to keep up their football.

This was why the boys greeted the headmaster's unexpected news at the end of the session with such excitement.

'I know you'll be glad of a change of scene,' he smiled. 'Jamie's father works at the new sports centre in Selworth and he's booked us in for some sessions on the all-weather pitches there.'

'Football under floodlights! Magic!' Chris enthused.

As they collected their coats, Pud collared Jamie. 'Why didn't you tell us earlier about the sports centre, eh, Gingernut?'

'My little secret,' he grinned impishly. 'Wanted it to be a surprise.'

'It sure was that, all right,' laughed Chris. 'What's this astro-turf like to play on, do you know?'

'Wicked! Dead flat, great for dribbling – as long as you've got the right kind of shoes.'

The players nearby looked down at their own feet. 'Aren't ordinary trainers any good?' asked Pud.

'You need special ones with better grip like I've got at home,' Jamie replied. 'Try to turn and shoot in those old things and you'll be flipped over on your back like a helpless tortoise!'

2 Floodlit Football

'Wow!' gasped Chris as Grandad pulled into the sports centre car park. 'Just look at all those lights.'

'Yeah, almost like daytime!' exclaimed Andrew, his elder brother, who had insisted on coming with them. 'Wish I could join in myself.'

Also in the car was Philip Smith, Danebridge's giraffe-like centre-back. 'Can't wait to try out my new trainers,' he babbled. 'Got them yesterday. Dad said I'd be sliding

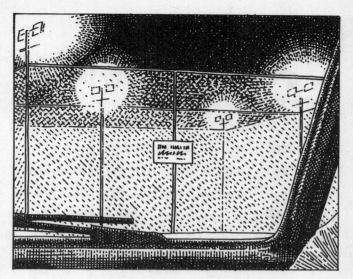

about all over the place otherwise.'

That was the one thing that was bothering Chris, but he tried to put it to the back of his mind. 'Hey! Look who's over there!' he cried as they walked towards the changing rooms. 'You see who I see, Phil?'

'Carl Diamond!' Philip groaned. 'Nobody could miss a head that size.'

'C'mon, he's not that bad, once you get to know him.'

Philip pulled a face. 'He still tries to

act the superstar too much for my liking. And I usually end up having to mark him!'

'Not tonight,' laughed Chris. 'He's with his Highgate squad.'

Andrew broke away from the group. 'Think I'll go and watch him for a bit, OK? While you lot get yourselves sorted out.'

'It wouldn't be because there's some teenage girls playing hockey nearby, would it, Andrew?' Grandad teased him.

'Is there?' he said innocently, colouring up. 'Hadn't even noticed.'

'I bet.' Chris grinned. 'Didn't know you were such a fan of Carl's.'

'I'm not. Just thought he might be able to get Dazzler Diamond's autograph for me. Best player in the

World Cup, his uncle was.'

'You'll be lucky. Probably have to wait till some big club pays millions to tempt him to leave Africa and come to play in this country.'

Philip tugged Chris's arm. 'C'mon, I'll have outgrown my new shoes by the time we get changed.'

As it was such a cold evening, Mr Jones organized a vigorous warm-up session for the whole squad before splitting the players up into groups to work on various skills. The activities allowed everyone to become more used to the green, sandy surface, twisting, turning and running with the ball.

Pud was the only reluctant participant. 'I'm not built for all this sprinting,' he grunted, breathing heavily between goes at dribbling a ball through a slalom arrangement of cones. 'When are we gonna have a game?'

Jamie ignored him, showing wonderful balance as he glided through the obstacle course with well-practised ease. He passed the ball on to the next player and Ryan set off eagerly, but a little too quickly for his own good. He lost possession of the ball to the second cone he met and then tripped up over the fifth, sprawling full length.

'Red card!' bellowed Pud. 'Send that cone off — deliberate foul!'

Ryan was glad to be wearing a tracksuit — not just as protection against the cold, but against the coarse tufts of artificial grass. Mr Jones had warned them of the danger of burn grazes, if any bare arms, elbows and legs came heavily into contact with the astro-turf.

The boy grinned with embarrassment as he picked himself up and carried on rather more steadily. He was one of the players whose trainers didn't have moulded, patterned soles for extra grip, and the early evening frost was already making some areas of the pitch quite slippery.

They were all pleased when the chance came to pull on their coloured training bibs for a seven-a-side game, Reds versus Yellows. Chris, in the

Yellows' goal, knew he had the weaker side in front of him, but he didn't mind that. It was bound to give him more practice – and keep him warmer!

He didn't expect to let a goal in with the first shot he faced, though – and especially not from Philip, as the big defender, more noted for his heading than his shooting, let fly from long range. The ball kept lower than Chris anticipated, skimming under his body into the goal.

'One—nil!' shouted Jamie. 'Easy! Easy!'

Chris ruefully picked the ball out of the tangled netting and resumed play by rolling it out to Jordan, the school's right-back. Jordan played a neat one-two pass with a teammate to start up a move that was finished by Pud hoofing a shot over the low crossbar at the other end.

'Stupid little goal,' Pud fumed. 'Why don't we play with proper ones?'

Chris was right about being kept busy. The lively Reds' attack of Jamie and Ryan caused his defence all sorts of problems. Without Chris, it might have been a massacre, but even he couldn't prevent Jamie helping himself to a hat-trick and supplying a couple of goals for Ryan.

Chris wasn't at all happy with his footwear. He'd slipped several times going for shots and failed to lay a glove on the ball. 'Have to get a pair of those special trainers,' he sighed. 'These are no good on here.'

Andrew came over to lean casually on the goalposts. 'Been talking to Carl,' he began. 'He says Selworth School come to train on here a lot, too, and I suggested you could all have a tournament together.'

'What, with just three schools?' snorted Chris.

'Why not?' said Andrew. 'It's called a triangular tournament.'

At that moment they saw Carl and the Highgate teacher heading towards Mr Jones. 'Guess they must have fancied the idea, anyway,' laughed Andrew. 'Be better than just practising here on your own, I reckon.'

'Hmm, a floodlit football tournament.' Chris nodded. 'I'm beginning to like the sound of that myself!'

'Are these for me?' Chris gasped.

Grandad chuckled with pleasure at Chris's excitement as the boy tore off his school shoes to try on the brand-new trainers. 'How do they feel?'

'Fantastic!' Chris whooped. 'Just perfect. Proper astro-turf ones! Thanks, Grandad, you're amazing. I'd no idea you were buying me these. I've been pestering Mum about some.'

'I know.' Grandad smiled, glancing out of his kitchen window at the snow-covered recreation ground. 'Want to go and try them out on the recky?'

Chris shook his head as he stamped

around on the tiled floor. 'No! Snow's too deep. Don't want to get them all messed up out there. I'll save their debut till the Sevens tournament starts tomorrow night.'

'Might be best. Andrew can wear his then as well.'

'He's not even playing,' Chris laughed. 'Have you got him a pair too?'

'Of course. Can't treat one and not the other, can I?' Grandad said. 'Who are you up against first in the Sevens?'

'Selworth, and then Highgate,' Chris answered. 'It's a round-robin type tournament, you know, where every team meets each other in a group. Only we're all going to do it twice over, playing next week as well!'

Grandad nodded slowly. 'I see – I think.'

'And then we're going to have a final play-off between the top two.'

'Good idea,' agreed Grandad. 'Gives you another game, that's the main thing – more practice.'

'If we make it to the play-off,' Chris added doubtfully. 'Selworth and Highgate are both more used to that all-weather surface than we are. They've got to be favourites.'

'Favourites don't always win,' Grandad said wisely, nudging Chris on the arm with his elbow and slipping him a wink.

3 Round-Robin

The following night the home town team of Selworth kicked off the floodlit triangular tournament. Looking cool — and braving the cold — in their light-blue shirts and matching tracksuit bottoms, they passed the ball around cleverly and confidently on the smooth surface.

'Get stuck in, Danebridge!' yelled Andrew from the side of the pitch. 'They're toying with you, making you look like dummies.'

Andrew felt frustrated, unable to go and put in a few crunching tackles himself. He'd already charged about in the warm-up in his new trainers, using his extra height and weight unfairly against the younger lads. Much to his annoyance, though, he had failed to score past his kid brother.

But Selworth did. Chris was well beaten by a firm drive and was grateful to see another effort clip the post and go out for a goal-kick. He clapped his gloved hands together – not so much to keep himself warm, as Selworth were already making things hot enough for him, but to urge his team on. 'C'mon the Reds!' he cried. 'Mark tighter.'

The Danebridge players were wearing the school's red, numbered bibs over their own tracksuits, and

the number five scratched his head in
bewilderment. 'How many men have
they got on the pitch?' Philip asked.
'Can't keep track of them all.'

'Same as us, Phil, just the seven,'
Chris assured him. 'I've already
counted!'

Chris kept them in the game with
two well-judged saves, but was left
stranded when Selworth did increase
the lead just before half-time. Their

captain and leading scorer, Dinesh, totally unmarked, had an easy tap-in goal to finish off a pacy move that sliced open the Danebridge defence.

Mr Jones reorganized their formation, bringing on a sub and asking Jamie to play deeper in midfield. 'That'll mean you, David, being up front on your own, I'm afraid, but see what you can do.'

Pud shrugged and saved his grumbles until he stood with Jamie, waiting to kick off the second period. 'Huh! Can't do anything if I don't get given the ball. The only times I've touched it is when we've done this.'

'They're showing us how to play on here,' Jamie replied. 'Keep the ball on the deck and knock it about, that's the way. Their players move real quick

into space for each other.'

'You getting at me, Titch?'

Jamie grinned. 'Well, you're not exactly the fastest thing on two legs, are you, Big Fellow?'

'What about you?' Pud snapped as the whistle blew. '*You* never pass the ball. You just dribble yourself inside out till you lose it.'

Pud was perhaps the most surprised player on the pitch when Jamie went and passed the ball straight back to him. 'Go on, then,' he said. 'There you are, you have it. Now what are you going to do with it?'

Pud never had chance to decide. He was robbed instantly and he waved his fist at Jamie's smirking face. When the ball did come his way again later, Pud was more prepared and demonstrated his shooting powers by rattling the Selworth crossbar. It was

Danebridge's first worthwhile shot of the game and Ryan was alert enough to snap up the loose ball and bundle it into the net.

The goal failed to spark off any comeback. The football traffic remained one-way, bearing down on Chris's area like a city centre in the rush hour. It was something of a minor miracle that no further goals were conceded — thanks partly to

Chris, but also to some large slices of luck.

'Good job our goal difference didn't suffer too much,' the headmaster said. 'Only lost two—one. They might have run up double figures.'

'I could do with a bit of a breather,' wheezed Philip. 'How much rest have we got, Mr Jones, before our next game?'

'None! You're back on straightaway. Highgate will be fresh and raring to go, but we can't play as badly as that again, surely.'

'Big effort, team!' Chris cried out from his goal before the match began. 'We just froze against Selworth.'

'Not surprising in this weather,' Philip said, wearing gloves like most of the players. 'But now we might catch Carl's lot cold at the start. They've been kept hanging around, shivering, waiting to come on.'

Philip's hopes were misplaced. Highgate were too good a team to be caught napping, but at least this game was more of an even contest. Each side enjoyed its fair share of attacking, scoring a goal apiece by half-time, with Carl not yet able to break free of Philip's shackles.

'You've been sticking so close to Carl, I thought you might even go and stand next to him during their team talk,' joked Jamie at the break.

Philip grinned. 'Good goal of yours, Little'un. A real fizzer!'

Only Chris wasn't satisfied with his own performance. 'Sorry about their equalizer, gang,' he murmured, shaking his head sadly. 'Just lost the ball somehow in the floodlights. I'll bring a cap next week so I don't get dazzled by them again.'

Two hard matches in succession, however, began to take their toll of the Danebridge energies. Legs grew tired, allowing Carl Diamond more freedom to stamp his class on the game. The tall black striker, an imposing figure in his all-white outfit, controlled most of Highgate's moves and it was no surprise when he put them ahead.

Carl received the ball in space as he sauntered over the halfway line, looked around as if to pass, and then decided to go it alone – as usual.

'Close him down!' Chris screamed. 'Don't let him run at you.'

Too late. Carl accelerated frighteningly fast, bursting past Ryan and Jamie, with the back-pedalling Philip in no position to challenge as Carl let

rip in full stride. Chris did well even to get a hand to the swirling shot before the ball buried itself in the netting behind him.

'C'mon, they haven't won yet,' Chris shouted. 'Fight back, men.'

If there was going to be a chance to hit back, Chris knew this was it. Teams sometimes went and let a soft goal in themselves straight after scoring, and now Highgate paid the price of falling for the sucker punch. While they were still dreaming of glory, Jamie was allowed to jink his way past two half-hearted tackles and level the scores once more.

Carl was furious with his players. 'You're useless!' he roared. 'You just let that little kid walk right through you.'

The sulking Carl seemed to lose interest in the game after that, but

Philip was well aware of Carl's moods. He knew the threat of danger was still there, like a simmering volcano that could suddenly blow its top and erupt into action.

And explode Carl did, without warning, surging forward with the ball in the very last seconds. Philip managed to block the first shot with his long outstretched leg, but Carl pounced again and scooped the rebound up towards the top corner. Chris flung himself to the right, straining his body just far enough to fingertip the ball over the bar.

The 2–2 draw left Danebridge with only a single point to show for their efforts. They stood huddled in coats around the pitch to watch the night's final game, not knowing what kind of result would suit them best.

In the end, however, Selworth felt just as helpless. They were made to look a shadow of the side that had so outplayed Danebridge earlier. Carl was determined to take his frustrations out on somebody and he simply blew them apart. It was a one-man wonder-show of soccer skills, and his superb hat-trick in a 3–1 victory fired Highgate to the top of the group table after the first round of games.

	P	W	D	L	F	A	Pts
Highgate	2	1	1	0	5	3	4
Selworth	2	1	0	1	3	4	3
Danebridge	2	0	1	1	3	4	1

4 Go for Goals

'Bottom of the table!' moaned Pud. 'We've got no chance of qualifying for the Final now.'

'Course we have,' Chris insisted. 'We've still got two more matches to play next week. Anything can happen yet.'

'Oh, yeah, sure! Selworth are too good for us, and if that bighead Carl turns it on, we've had it.'

'Rubbish!' scoffed Philip. 'Football doesn't work like that. Every game's different. Just needs a bit of skill or luck or . . .'

'Or somebody not falling over when they should have scored!' Jamie chipped in, glancing sidelong in Pud's direction. He was ready to bolt across the snow-covered playground if Pud made a sudden grab for him.

'Can't help it if I slipped,' Pud said in disgust. They might even have beaten Highgate, if his left foot hadn't slid away as he prepared to hit a master-blaster with his right. 'My trainers have worn too smooth and we can't afford any new ones.'

It was a serious problem that Chris had already considered. They needed Pud's firepower up front, but he'd been almost like a passenger so far, unable to keep his feet when trying to turn on the artificial surface.

'What size do you take?' he asked.

43

'Sevens, why?'

'Sevens!' Jamie gasped. 'Mine are only twos. Pud must be a Bigfoot!'

They all laughed as Pud reddened, but Chris managed to smooth his ruffled feathers. 'It's OK, Pud, forget it. I think I know somebody who might just be able to help us out . . .'

The following week Andrew stood grumpily on the sidelines in his old trainers. It had cost Chris half his pocket money to bribe his brother to lend his new ones, but he considered the sacrifice worthwhile. At least, that is, if they helped Pud to move about properly.

'No sweat! I'll be all right now,' Pud beamed. 'And, anyway, even if I'm not, Jonesy's got nobody else to replace me!'

Danebridge had lost their substitute.

A phone message informed them that his dad's car had spun into a ditch on an icy country road. Nobody was hurt, but the car was out of action and the boy couldn't play.

Despite this setback, Danebridge's evening got off to a flying start and the captain's expensive gamble paid off sooner than he dared hope.

Jordan's long clearance found Pud deep in Selworth territory and it looked at first as if the striker was winding himself up to shoot. Feeling more confident with his better grip, however, Pud knocked the ball further on instead. He let the nearest challenger bounce off him and then crashed the ball goalwards. The keeper, Aaron, got both hands to the ball — and immediately regretted it. His pain was made worse by seeing the ball spinning around in the bottom of the net.

Selworth had expected to win comfortably again, but this time met with far more determined resistance. Defenders Philip, Jordan and Tom tackled like tanks, Ryan and Jamie worked hard in midfield and, behind them all, Chris was in top form. He stopped anything that escaped his teammates, making save after save, and it wasn't until late in the game that Selworth finally scored a deserved equalizer. A half-hit shot was turned wide of a wrong-footed Chris by the lurking Dinesh.

'Tough luck,' said Aaron as the two goalkeepers shook hands after the 1–1 draw. 'Thought we'd never get the ball past you tonight.'

Chris tried to rally his troops. 'Right, team, we've just shown how well we can play on here. If we can get three points by beating Highgate, we'll leap-frog above them and Selworth in the group.'

'They've got to play each other yet, remember,' Philip put in.

'OK, but they can't both win, can they? Every goal could be crucial. It might all come down to goal difference, if we're level on points.'

'So what are we waiting for?' cried Pud. 'Let's go for goals!'

That was much easier said than done. Danebridge failed to score at all in the first half and trailed 1–0 as they changed ends.

'You lot are history!' Carl Diamond taunted them. 'You might as well pack up your gear and go home. It's just between us and Selworth now.'

It did look that way. Chris knew that even a draw would be of no use. It was win or bust. 'C'mon, team,' he called out. 'If you want to play another match – and shut his big mouth – it's got to be all-out attack this half.'

Highgate's goal still rankled with Chris. He didn't like letting one in at the best of times, but the way Carl had scored made it even worse. The striker had slammed into little Jamie with bone-jarring force to win the ball, sending him sprawling backwards across the hard surface. The Danebridge players appealed in vain

for a foul. To their amazement, the referee waved play on, allowing Carl to elbow Tom aside as well before steering his shot under the diving Chris.

Jamie nursed a personal grudge, too, and wanted to exact revenge on Carl in the manner that he knew would hurt the most. Not physically, but mentally – by making him taste defeat.

First, however, Carl almost put the game beyond Danebridge's reach. He muscled his way past Philip and sent a left-footed curler towards goal. A cry of triumph had to be stifled in his throat as, for once, the keeper's ability matched his own. Chris managed to get his body right behind the line of the ball and clutched it safely to his chest.

Shortly afterwards, Danebridge levelled the scores – and then went in front themselves: two goals in a minute that killed Highgate off, a double blow from which they were unable to recover.

Though none of his own team would have dared to do it, fingers of blame deserved to be pointed at the Highgate captain for the equalizer. It was a sweet moment that Jamie relished, seizing his chance to catch Carl off guard. As Carl sidestepped a challenge from Jordan on the halfway line, Jamie sneaked up from behind to nip the ball off his toes.

Carl aimed a wild kick at Jamie but he was gone, whipping a pass out to Ryan on the wing and calling for the return. When it came, it was too far in front of Jamie but the ball ran into Pud's path instead and he walloped it home. The keeper had no chance to prevent the second either as Ryan was put through by Tom to net the decisive goal.

Carl's shrieks of complaint at his teammates were so embarrassing that Highgate's teacher subbed him. That was the last straw for Carl. He snatched up his bag and headed for the changing rooms and the teacher made no attempt to stop him.

Danebridge's 2–1 victory assured their place in the Final. 'We're one point clear of the other teams and with a better goal difference than Selworth,' Mr Jones explained. 'So even if this last match ends in a draw, we'll still qualify.'

Pud had a nasty thought. 'But what if Selworth win?'

'We'd still be better off than Highgate,' the headmaster smiled.

'Extra maths for you tomorrow, David, I think, to work out league tables!'

Selworth did win, handsomely, taking full advantage of the missing Carl. The previous week's hat-trick hero had disappeared, rumoured to have gone home early in a huff, unable to face up to the humiliation.

Without their self-appointed superstar, the dispirited Highgate team slumped to a heavy 4–0 defeat, leaving them bottom of the group. The scene was now set for a Selworth–Danebridge Final.

	P	W	D	L	F	A	Pts
Selworth	4	2	1	1	8	5	7
Danebridge	4	1	2	1	6	6	5
Highgate	4	1	1	2	6	9	4

5 Shot in the Dark

'How are the trainers, Pud?' Andrew asked in the short rest break before the Final.

'Wicked! Think I'll keep them.'

'No way! They're on loan for one night only. Just make sure you don't damage them. Do you have to kick the ball so hard?'

'Yes, he does,' Chris butted in. 'Captain's orders! I want to see him warming that Selworth keeper's hands again.'

'I can't get the same power in these as my soccer boots,' Pud admitted. 'Give me real grass to play on any day.'

'You might not have too long to wait, then,' Andrew said.

'What do you mean?' asked Chris eagerly, pulling on his goalie gloves.

'Grandad's been inside to warm up a bit and heard the latest weather forecast. They reckon the big freeze is over. We're in for a thaw!'

It certainly didn't feel like it at the moment for the players. 'Forget the cold,' Mr Jones told them. 'Go out and enjoy this last game. Whatever the result, let's see you play some good football.'

The boys took him at his word. They were very keen to win the tournament, but wanted to show off a few of their new skills too. They had not been slow to learn how to play on the flat, all-weather surface and now gave Selworth as good as they got. It rained goals.

The Danebridge defence was the first to leak. Dinesh found a hole through the middle and Chris's brave block failed to prevent the ball trickling over the line. Then Selworth were in need of a brolly! Jamie, Pud and Ryan poured forward in search of the equalizer, linking up smoothly to allow Ryan to lash a shot past Aaron from close range.

The same player scored their second goal too, edging Danebridge in front after a clever free-kick routine. As Jamie ran over the ball, Pud lumbered up behind and Aaron's trembling wall of bodies braced themselves for the expected blast. Instead, Pud merely tapped the ball to his left

to give Ryan a clear sight of goal. He made no mistake.

That was when Danebridge's luck ran out. Just before the half-time breather, Jordan twisted over on his ankle as he went to make a tackle and crumpled up into a heap. The ever-alert Dinesh darted into the vacant space, demanding the ball. He got it, looked up and took aim, but his shot was going wide of the target until it struck Tom.

It was a cruel moment of misfortune for the defender. Tom had sprinted across goal to cover and could not get out of the way in time. The ball hit him on the knee and whistled past Chris to level the scores again.

'Do you want to carry on, Jordan?' the headmaster asked.

The boy nodded. 'Got to. There's no sub.'

'Doesn't matter. We'll just have to be one player short.'

Jordan insisted he was all right, but as he hobbled back onto the pitch for the second half, it was clear that he would not be able to play a full part in the game. His teammates knew they were up against it now, but Chris remained optimistic that his weakened side might yet conjure up a victory. And they did have their chances. Pud blazed one over the bar, Jamie screwed a shot wide after a wonderful dribble and Ryan missed a golden opportunity to bag a hat-trick.

Selworth were wasteful, too, and even Dinesh was guilty of losing his cool in front of goal. He fooled Philip by nutmegging the gangly centre-back, slipping the ball through his legs, but seemed to panic when faced by Chris and hammered it straight at the grateful keeper.

A minute later the two captains confronted each other again in a one-against-one duel. Jordan's lack of mobility allowed Dinesh to snap up a loose ball and cut inside for goal. He was tempted to try and dribble round Chris this time, but was still confident enough to have another shot.

As Dinesh drew back his foot to strike the ball, the lights went out.

Chris was aware of something whizzing past his head and then heard the dreaded sound of the net rippling behind him. Lots of shouts and screams rang out at the same time as the whole sports arena had been suddenly plunged into darkness. Total confusion reigned.

'Is everybody OK?'

'Don't be frightened.'

'What's happened?'

'All the floodlights have failed.'

'Must be a power cut.'

'It's these freezing temperatures.'

As Chris grew accustomed to the gloom, he saw the ball lying in the net and Dinesh leading his teammates in a wild dance of celebration.

'Hey! Hang on a minute!' the Danebridge captain called out. 'I didn't even see it.'

Pud complained loudly to the Highgate teacher who was refereeing the Final. 'C'mon, ref, that ain't fair! You can't count that.'

'No need to act like Carl, lad,' the teacher grinned. 'Don't worry, it's no goal. And if the lights don't come back on soon, there will be no more football tonight either!'

Some of the Selworth party made

feeble protests about the goal being disallowed, but most people saw it was the only sensible decision. Even so, Danebridge were the ones who finished up feeling frustrated.

After waiting a quarter of an hour, the floodlights remained off and the match was abandoned as a draw. Selworth, though, were declared the tournament winners for topping the group.

'Never mind, lads, you did your-selves proud,' said the headmaster as the players collected their belongings from the chilly changing rooms. 'It's not the end of the world. There's still lots of soccer left to catch up on this season.'

'Do you know what match we've got first, Mr Jones?' Chris asked.

'Yes, I arranged it this evening in fact,' he chuckled. 'It's at home, once the pitch is fit. And you've been seeing quite a lot of your opponents recently . . .'

'Not Highgate, I hope,' muttered Jamie, thinking of Carl.

'Can't be,' said Chris. 'We've already played them in the league.'

As the penny dropped, the room was in uproar. 'It'll be great to get

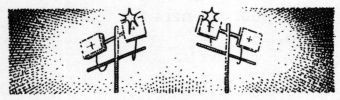

Selworth back on our own muddy recky,' grinned Philip. 'But I bet *they* won't be looking forward to it!'

'Yeah,' agreed Ryan, 'I reckon we would have gone on to beat them, if it hadn't been for this stupid power cut.'

'Dead right, there,' grunted Pud, taking off the trainers. 'They know we've still got a score to settle with 'em.'

Andrew moved in before Pud forgot about something in the excitement. 'Mine, I think,' he said, easing his trainers out of Pud's grip.

6 The Real Thing

'I'd almost forgotten what grass looked like!'

'Incredible how green it is!'

'Bet it'll feel weird playing on it again after that artificial stuff.'

The footballers were gazing over their small playing field next to the school. Patches of grass were beginning to show through the melting mounds of slushy ice and snow as the winter sunshine got on with its work.

'Won't be long now before we can play some *real* football,' Philip said.

'Real football?' queried Chris. 'What do you think we've been playing under floodlights – tiddlywinks?'

'We all know what he means,' said Pud. 'Can hardly wait till these lumps of snow have gone and I get my trusty old shooting boots on again.'

'No need to wait, if you don't want to,' Jamie replied. 'We could just use you as a heavy roller to flatten out the recky pitch.'

Jamie darted away to a safer distance as Pud made a move towards him. 'Imagine Pud all covered in snow,' he chortled. 'He wouldn't be Bigfoot any longer – he'd be the Abominable Snowman!'

That did it. Pud gave chase across the playground and they disappeared round the corner of the building –

straight into the patrolling head-master. All three of them finished in a soggy heap on the mushy tarmac.

'Er, sorry, Mr Jones,' Jamie began hesitantly, trying to suppress any giggles as the headmaster struggled back onto his feet. 'Just . . . er . . .'

Pud finished the excuse for him. 'Just proving to Freckles here — I mean, Jamie — that I can be quicker off the mark than he thinks!'

Mr Jones grimaced at the dirt all down the side of his clothes. 'Well, let's see how quickly you can both go round to my office now – *walking*!'

A week later, on a bright Saturday morning in February, Danebridge School's league soccer season was due to kick off again on the recky.

Unfortunately the frost had returned suddenly overnight. The grass was white-over and the ground hard and crisp underfoot. Mr Jones had warned the players about the bad weather forecast and they came prepared. Chris wouldn't be the only one wearing tracksuit bottoms and gloves.

'Is the game still on?' Chris asked when he arrived. He was desperate to play, despite the fact that he was starting a cold.

Philip grinned. 'Jonesy's already inspected the pitch and said it's playable. Got your all-weather trainers?'

Chris nodded, wiping his nose. 'And my cap. The sun's really low and dazzly this morning. Worse than those floodlights!'

Mr Jones gathered everyone together. 'It'll be good experience for you today in these conditions,' he told them. 'I'm afraid the pitch is too hard to take a stud, though. You'd be falling over all the time in boots.'

'Only got my old trainers,' Pud muttered to Chris.

'Sorry, Pud,' he apologized. 'Couldn't borrow Andrew's again. He needed them himself for his own school match this morning.'

Pud shrugged. 'I'll be OK, don't bother. Just keep picking me up!'

Grandad spoke to Chris from his favourite spot, leaning against his back garden wall. 'The surface is pretty bumpy and rutted so watch the bounce! Hmm, you don't look too good, m'boy. How are you feeling?'

'OK, Grandad, thanks,' Chris replied, unable to hide a sniffle.

Grandad looked at him hard. 'Does your mother know about this cold?'

Chris shook his head. 'Just woke up with it this morning.'

'Aye, well, take care. May the best team win, as I always say.'

'As long as it's us, eh?' grinned Chris.

There was a lot of banter between the Danebridge and Selworth squads in the wooden changing hut. This league match was very important to them, in terms of both pride and points, and the players were keyed up for it.

Dinesh won the toss and decided to kick towards the River Dane. 'Just to give you the sun in your eyes first half!' he smirked at Chris.

The goalkeeper shrugged. 'Fine, no problem. I'll be able to get a sun tan while old Aaron's kept busy picking the ball out of his net.'

Ball control was difficult on the firm, frosty ground, but the two sides still tried to play the same kind of skilful, passing game as in the Sevens. Grandad smiled, pleased to see Danebridge showing better teamwork now after their weeks of practice indoors and under lights.

He was even more delighted when

their opening goal came from a typical piece of patient, stylish play along the left touchline. The move began with an accurate throw from Chris out to Tom in space, who then swapped passes with Ryan and Jamie until the little winger was sent clear with only a single defender barring his path.

Jamie sold the boy a classic dummy, leaving him on the seat of his pants just like the headmaster in the playground. He then took on Aaron as well, shimmying neatly round the keeper and sidefooting the ball home.

Danebridge's lead didn't last long. Selworth's own efforts were rewarded before half-time with an equally well-taken goal. Their nimble forwards skated over the bobbly surface as if

they were back on the astro-turf, and Dinesh tucked the ball inside Chris's far post with great glee.

'C'mon, we're not going to let them beat us on our home patch,' Pud growled at the break. 'Let's get stuck into them, I'm goal-starved.'

'Oh, no! Pud's getting hungry again,' Jamie joked. 'Watch out, Selworth, the Abominable *Slow*-man is coming to gobble you up!'

Even Pud had to laugh and team spirits were high as they forced several quick corners at the start of the second half. Jamie swung the right-wing ones into the penalty area with his left foot and Pud drilled them across from the other side. The sound of Pud ploughing through the frosty layers of crunchy, crackling leaves near the corner flag was even louder than the noises he made in the school hall at lunch with his packets of crisps.

The deserved goal came not from Philip's head, but from the unlikely source of Jordan's. The full-back, his ankle no longer sore, timed his run perfectly to glance one of Jamie's deadly inswingers past the groping goalkeeper. It was Jordan's first-ever goal for the school.

Danebridge strangely relaxed their grip on the game after this, though, and Selworth took control. It was the turn of Chris's goal to face a period of bombardment, but the visitors came up against an inspired keeper.

Chris always relished being in the thick of the action and he forgot all about his runny nose: he was enjoying himself too much. When he emerged with the ball again, plastered with dirt from another mad scramble, his goalmouth looked as if it had been trampled by a whole family of Yeti!

He kicked the ball away upfield to gain a bit of a breathing space, and it reached Pud, who was parked in the slippery centre-circle. The number nine turned with difficulty and nearly fell as he bumbled forwards, looking around for help. For once, it wasn't there. All the other Danebridge players had been back in defence, trying to prevent a second equalizer.

Pud found himself confronted by two defenders and a long run towards goal. He didn't fancy it, knowing he'd easily get caught. Glancing up, he saw that Aaron was positioned right out near the edge of the penalty area and felt tempted to have a go. The goalkeeper never imagined that

anybody would even think of shooting from such a range. He was wrong.

Pud steadied himself, set his sights and then whacked the ball hard and high. It came out of the sun's glare and sailed goalwards, bang on target, and the keeper knew he was beaten. Aaron made a half-hearted attempt to get back, but could only watch as the ball soared over his head and plopped down, one bounce, into the billowing net.

The scorer was the only person on the recky not to see the amazing goal. As he struck the ball, Pud's standing foot had skidded from underneath him and he finished up spread-eagled on his back, winded and staring up into the clear blue sky. He lay there with a silly grin across his chubby face, too heavy for anyone to lift up, but there was plenty of him for his

laughing teammates to hug once he'd
regained his feet!

Five minutes later the match was
all over and Danebridge's 3–1 win

kept them at the top of the league table. Already the boys were starting to dream – and chant – about winning the championship and the changing hut was too noisy a place for Grandad. He retired to his cosy kitchen.

He was on his second cup of tea by the time his grandson finally appeared in the doorway. 'Champions!' Chris croaked.

'Aye, maybe, but there's a long way to go yet,' Grandad chuckled. 'Come and sit down and get warm. I'll pour you a hot drink.'

Chris suddenly whipped out his hankie. 'Aaahh-chooo!!'

'Bless you, m'boy!' said Grandad. 'Well, I don't know, the big freeze might nearly be over at last, but now we've got the big sneeze!'

THE END